I WANT EVERYTHING!

BY ALBERTO PELLAI &
BARBARA TAMBORINI

ILLUSTRATED BY
ELISA PAGANELLI

I WANT THE MOON AS MY KICKBALL,
SNOW IN THE SUMMER, AND
THE SOUND OF THE OCEAN AS MY LULLABY!

YOU THINK THAT TRICYCLE IS YOURS?
IT'S NOT. IT'S MINE.
I'M THE KING OF EVERYTHING, NOT YOU.

IF I WANT TO BE A LION, I WILL ROAR LIKE A LION.

But you are acting rude when you roar like a lion
and frighten everyone with your angry voice.

OK, FINE. IF I CAN'T ROAR, THEN I'LL TAKE THEIR NECK, TRUNK, AND STRIPES. EVERYTHING IS MINE.

Really? A giraffe without a long neck can't reach leaves in the tree. An elephant without his trunk can't eat grass. And a tiger without stripes is too sad to hunt.

WELL, I'M HUNGRY. I WANT LUNCH.

WHAT? LIONS DON'T EAT SOUP. I DON'T WANT THIS.

Soup is good for hungry lions. Nutritious and calming, fit for a king. Do you think Tiger, Giraffe, or Elephant might want it instead?

OK. FINE. I AM HUNGRY. I WILL EAT THIS LUNCH SO I CAN PLAY.

LOOK. I MADE THIS PARK FOR MY FRIENDS.
WE PLAYED HIDE-AND-SEEK.
BUT MONKEY LOST HIS HAT ON THE ROLLERCOASTER.

What fun! Almost time for bed,
so soon you need to clean up.

I CAN'T, I CAN'T, I WANT TO WATCH TV!

If you clean up *quickly*,
there is still time to watch TV before bedtime.

OK. FINE. MONKEY WILL HELP ME.

It's night, and time for bed.
All of the animals are at home.

I WANT TO STAY UP ALL NIGHT WITH THE OWLS. I DON'T
WANT TO GO TO BED.

Little lions need to rest...

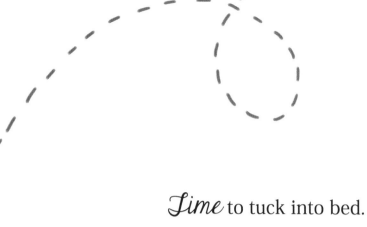

Time to tuck into bed.

I will sing you a song
that will fly with you through your dreams.

And my little lion, the stars will roar for you.

It's time to sleep, *good night*.

Reader's Note

The management of whims and tantrums is a real challenge for parents. Children make seemingly random decisions about what they need or want, and break down when they don't get it. A common struggle for children between 3 and 6 years old is a belief in their own omnipotence: "If I want something I have to have it! If I don't want to, I don't have to!" Adults need to teach children to tolerate some frustration and to regulate their emotions. The key is knowing how to mix kindness and firmness depending on the situation.

Remain Calm. It is important that the adult remains calm, gives the child time to let the emotions flow, and remains in sight, even if at a distance. It's easy to get frustrated, but the adult is the one who needs to calm the situation. Children take their cues from us; we have to set a good example.

Set Firm Limits. The challenge for the parent is to be able to say "no" firmly and calmly, and to stick to it. True freedom and healthy emotional development comes from the ability to tolerate frustrations, to learn to negotiate and to see more than just their own vision of the world. If the child does not want to follow your rules, you must not give in, or they won't take the rule seriously. Better to limit yourself to a few rules that you are strict about than to have many that you can't always enforce. Similarly, try not to promise exaggerated punishments that you can't stick to ("no TV for a month!"). Better to have smaller, but realistic, consequences ("you're going to lose TV time after dinner tonight").

Prepare in Advance. Who knows your children better than you? You know what they love to do and when they find it more difficult to follow the rules. You know when they're more likely to break down. The best way you can help is to prevent trantrums before they begin. Establishing firm routines ahead of time is one of the best ways to do this. If, for example, the child often throws a tantrum about having to sit at the dinner table, establish expectations ahead of time: "You have to sit at least ten minutes."

Help Them Find Calm. It's nearly impossible for the child to absorb any new information when they are in the middle of a tantrum, so try practicing the calming strategies when they are already calm. That way they have a better chance of retaining them and are more likely to be able to use them when upset. These actions can be as simple as hiding their head in their arms, taking deep breaths, or hugging a stuffed toy tight. Maybe they just need some time by themselves to cool down. You can also help them find a space at home where they can take refuge when they feel anger overwhelming them.

Validate Their Achievements. The rules must be few and logical, and make space for a reward. The child is more likely to respect them and follow them if they are consistently enforced and open a possibility for reward. For example, "As long as you put them away after, you can play with all the games you want."

ALBERTO PELLAI, MD, PhD, is a child psychotherapist and a researcher at the Department of Bio-medical Sciences of the University of Milan. In 2004, the Ministry of Health awarded him the silver medal of merit for public health. He is the author of numerous books for parents, teachers, teenagers, and children.
He lives in Italy.
Visit albertopellailibri.it
@alberto_pellai

BARBARA TAMBORINI is a psycho-pedagogist and writer. She leads workshops in schools for teachers and parents. She is the author with Alberto Pellai of several books aimed at parents. She lives in Somma, Italy.
@Barbara Tamborini

ELISA PAGANELLI is an award-winning illustrator and freelance designer.
She attended the Institute of Art and subsequently graduated in illustration from the European Institute of Design (IED) in Turin. Since, she has worked on over a hundred children's books. Elisa lives in the UK.
Visit elisapaganelli.com
@ElisaPaganelliillustrator
@elisaupsidedown
@elisapaganelli_illustration

MAGINATION PRESS is the children's book imprint of the American Psychological Association. Through APA's publications, the association shares with the world mental health expertise and psychological knowledge. Magination Press books reach young readers and their parents and caregivers to make navigating life's challenges a little easier. It's the combined power of psychology and literature that makes a Magination Press book special.
Visit www.maginationpress.org
@maginationpress

Books for Kids From the American Psychological Association

Original Title: Voglio Tutto, Sono un Re!
World copyright © 2017 DeA Planeta Libri S.r.l.

Magination Press is a registered trademark of the American Psychological Association. Order books at maginationpress.org, or call 1-800-374-2721.

English translation by Katie ten Hagen
Book design by Rachel Ross
Printed by Worzalla, Stevens Point, WI

Cataloging-in-Publication data is on file at the Library of Congress.
ISBN-13: 978-1-4338-3242-0
LCCN: 2019055232

Manufactured in the United States of America
10 9 8 7 6 5 4 3 2 1